Lily and the Mixed-Up Letters

DEBORAH HODGE

Illustrated by

FRANCE BRASSARD

Tundra Books

Published in Canada by Tundra Books,
75 Sherbourne Street, Toronto, Ontario M5A 2P9

Published in the United States by Tundra Books of Northern New York,
P.O. Box 1030, Plattsburgh, New York 12901

Library of Congress Control Number: 2006925483

Library and Archives Canada Cataloguing in Publication

Hodge, Deborah
    Lily and the mixed-up letters / Deborah Hodge ; illustrated by
France Brassard.

ISBN 978-0-88776-757-9

    1. Dyslexia—Juvenile fiction. I. Brassard, France, 1963– II. Title.

PS8565.O295L54 2007   jC813'.6   C2006-902066-3

We acknowledge the financial support of the Government of Canada through the Book
Publishing Industry Development Program (BPIDP) and that of the Government of
Ontario through the Ontario Media Development Corporation's Ontario Book
Initiative. We further acknowledge the support of the Canada Council for the Arts and
the Ontario Arts Council for our publishing program.

The illustrations for this book were rendered in watercolor on Arches paper.
Design: Kong Njo

Printed and bound in China

1 2 3 4 5 6   12 11 10 09 08 07

For Helen, my very own Lily,
and for Dave, Mike, and Pete,
some of the smartest people I know.
– D.H.

To my son, Luke,
who is learning the magic of reading.
– F.B.

Lily used to love school.

When she was in kindergarten, she dressed up in the costume corner and acted out stories with her friends. She made playdough animals at the modeling table. She sang all the songs at music time and ran as fast as she could in the gym.

But Lily's favorite thing to do was to paint big, bright pictures. She painted flowers and her family and her best friend, Grace. She painted the baby lambs on her cousin's farm and her furry old dog, Max. She painted the sky and the mountains and the kids in her neighborhood.

"Your paintings are beautiful!" everyone said.

Now, Lily's in grade 2 and school isn't fun anymore. Her mom calls, "Wake up, Lily. It's time for school."

"I have a sick stomach," says Lily. "My head hurts. I can't go."

"You said that yesterday," says her mom, "and you felt fine by the afternoon. I think you should go today."

Lily takes a long time to get dressed and even longer to eat her breakfast.

At school, it's time for reading. Lily takes her book out of her desk. She likes the pictures but the words don't make any sense. When she tries to sound them out, the letters dance and blur in front of her eyes. Her head pounds. She tries and tries, but she just can't read the words.

The kids take turns reading out loud. Grace can read the words. So can the other kids. But when it's Lily's turn, her face grows hot and her hands get shaky. Her stomach turns upside down. She feels everyone watching her.

"I have a sore throat," she tells the teacher, "I can't read today." Then she puts her head down on the desk.

When the recess bell goes, the kids race outside. Lily feels much better. She gobbles up her snack and plays tag with Grace and the other kids.

After recess, the teacher makes an announcement. Parent Day is next week! All the parents will come to school. The kids will get ready by decorating the class with paintings and practicing their reading. On Parent Day, each child will read a page from their book.

Lily feels a knot in her stomach. How will she read her page?

The kids get out their books to practice. Lily stares and stares at her page, but the letters get all mixed up and so does she. Her lip starts to quiver. Her eyes fill with tears. Lily hides her face so the teacher won't see.

When it's time for art, Lily goes straight to the painting table. She paints picture after picture.

"I love your kitten," says Grace, watching Lily paint. "Can you show me how to paint like that?"

Grace's kitten isn't anything like Lily's. Grace looks sad.

"You'll get it," Lily says, smiling. "You just need to practice."

When school ends, the kids take home invitations to Parent Day. They take their books, too, so they can practice their pages. Lily stuffs hers in the bottom of her backpack.

That evening, when Lily is helping with the dishes, she is very quiet.

"Is something wrong?" asks her mom.

Lily's shoulders begin to shake and tears run down her face. "I can't do it," she sobs. "I can't read my page on Parent Day. It's too hard. All the other kids can read their pages, but I can't read mine."

Her mom wraps her arms around Lily and holds her close. "I'm sorry," she says. Her eyes get shiny. After a long pause, she says, "It was hard for me, too. I couldn't read much until I was ten."

"Really?" says Lily. She is surprised. She knows her mom has no trouble now, because she reads bedtime stories every night. Lily wants to read like her.

"I'll talk to your teacher," says her mom, "and ask her to give you extra help in reading."

At school the next day, Lily looks at her page. She still doesn't know the words, but Grace comes to help her learn them.

"I'm going to be your reading buddy," says Grace.

"Okay," says Lily, "and I'll be your painting buddy."

Lily and Grace sit together. When Lily can't figure out a word, she asks Grace to tell it to her. Lily says each word over and over. She says them fast, she says them slow. She makes a song of them. Every day that week, she practices her page. Sometimes, she even stays in at lunch to work on it.

Every night that week, she takes her book home. She practices before dinner and after dinner. Her mom shows her tricks for remembering the words. Lily draws them big in the air. She writes them in colored pencils. She closes her eyes tight and paints them on the easel in her mind. Over and over, one word at a time. Lily works harder and longer on her page than anyone else in the class.

Before she knows it, Parent Day is here. When Lily and her mom get to school, the parents are looking at the painting display. A group is gathered around Lily's paintings.

"These are amazing," someone says. Lily beams.

The parents watch the kids in the sharing circle, then at printing and math. Finally, it's time to read. First it's Alyssa, then Sam, Matthew, and Grace.

Now, it's Lily's turn. She walks to the front. Her legs are weak and wobbly. The book slips in her wet hands. Everything on her page goes blurry. Lily freezes. The room is silent. Everyone's waiting.

Lily closes her eyes as tight as she can. She thinks about how hard she's practiced. She hunts for the words in the back of her mind. Then, she takes a big breath, opens her eyes, and begins to read.

At first, her voice is low and slow. She reads the first sentence and gets most of it right. Her voice gets a little louder. She stumbles over a word in the next sentence, but she doesn't stop. Lily's reading isn't as smooth or as fast as the other kids' and she makes mistakes. But she keeps on going, word after word and sentence after sentence, until . . . she reads the whole page!

Everyone claps as Lily walks
back to her desk. Her mom gives
her a huge hug.
"You did it!" she says.

The parents and kids eat a special lunch together. Lily and Grace sit at the same table.

"I'm going to be an artist when I grow up," says Lily.

"I'm going to be a teacher," says Grace.

"And, we'll still be best friends," they say, laughing.

"You were great today." says Lily's mom. "I'm so proud of you."

Lily smiles. She's proud of herself, too. She sees that reading is hard for her and she has to practice way more than the other kids. But, she did it today and she knows she can do it again.

Feeling as light as a kite on the wind,
Lily skips all the way home.